RETURN TO THE
LIBRARY OF DOOM

THE SEA OF LOST BOOKS

BY MICHAEL DAHL

ILLUSTRATED BY
BRADFORD KENDALL

STONE ARCH BOOKS
a capstone imprint

ZONE BOOKS ARE PUBLISHED BY
STONE ARCH BOOKS
A CAPSTONE IMPRINT
151 GOOD COUNSEL DRIVE, P.O. BOX 669
MANKATO, MINNESOTA 56002
WWW.CAPSTONEPUB.COM

LIBRARY OF CONGRESS CATALOGING-IN-PUBLICATION DATA
DAHL, MICHAEL.
   THE SEA OF LOST BOOKS / WRITTEN BY MICHAEL DAHL ;
ILLUSTRATED BY BRADFORD KENDALL.
        P. CM. -- (RETURN TO THE LIBRARY OF DOOM)
   ISBN 978-1-4342-2142-1 (LIBRARY BINDING)
  (1. ROBBERS AND OUTLAWS--FICTION. 2. BOOKS AND READING--
FICTION. 3. HORROR STORIES.) I. KENDALL, BRADFORD, ILL. II.
TITLE.
   PZ7.D15134SE 2010
   (FIC)--DC22   2010004057

ART DIRECTOR: KAY FRASER
GRAPHIC DESIGNER: HILARY WACHOLZ
PRODUCTION SPECIALIST: MICHELLE BIEDSCHEID

Chapter 1:
THE SUNKEN ROOMS 6

Chapter 2:
FLOATING TREASURE 12

Chapter 3:
ATLAS 19

Chapter 4:
DEADLY LETTERS 29

Chapter 5:
FINAL PAPER 37

Chapter 6:
ENTER, THE SPECIALIST 48

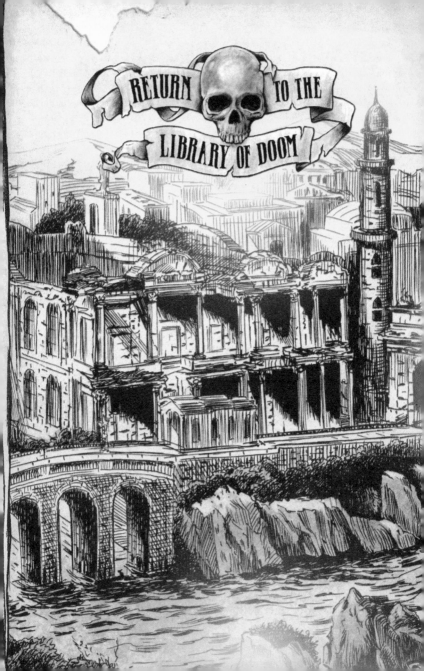

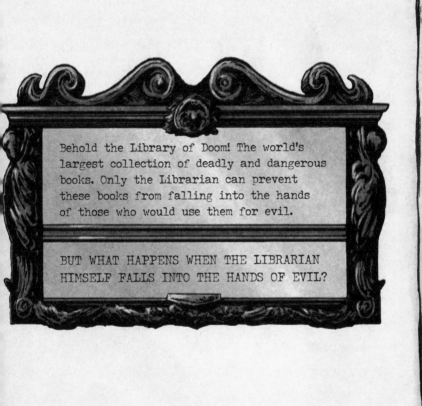

Behold the Library of Doom! The world's largest collection of deadly and dangerous books. Only the Librarian can prevent these books from falling into the hands of those who would use them for evil.

BUT WHAT HAPPENS WHEN THE LIBRARIAN HIMSELF FALLS INTO THE HANDS OF EVIL?

Chapter 1

THE SUNKEN ROOMS

At the edge of the Library of Doom, a dark sea roars.

Part of the library is built beneath the WAVES.

Underwater rooms HOLD shelves of books.

The books are made of jewels, coral, and pearls.

Sharks guard the watery rooms of the library.

They prowl between the shelves of books. They patrol the **SILENT** rooms.

Their mouths are full of razor-sharp **TEETH**.

A light **glows**.

The sharks stop swimming.

Their eyes fill with **fear**.

A shadow glides through the sea.

The sharks **FLEE**.

The shape moves toward the underwater rooms.

Long arms STRETCH through the water.

Each arm is full of poison.

The arms reach out toward the library.

Chapter 2

FLOATING TREASURE

The arms **WRAP** around the library's windows and towers.

Then the arms tighten.

They SQUEEZE hard.

The library rooms are **crushed**.

The walls shatter.

Books stream through the cracks.

They rush out like schools of
frightened fish.

The books **float** higher. Soon, they reach the surface of the sea.

They lie on the waves like flat, square islands.

The *shadow* moves beneath the floating books.

Glowing arms reach into the air. The arms belong to a **monstrous** jellyfish.

A huge air bubble floats at the center of the **JELLYFISH**.

Inside the bubble stands a GIGANTIC man.

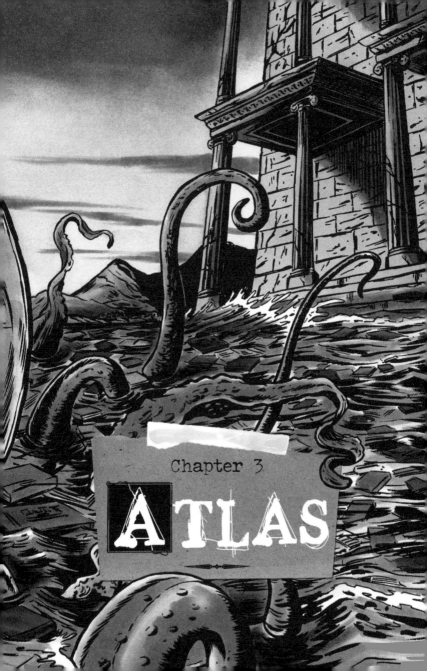

Chapter 3

ATLAS

The bubble rises higher. It **RIDES** on the waves.

The giant steps out of the bubble. He **steps** onto the floating books.

His body is covered with tattoos.

Each tattoo is a <u>letter</u>.

Across his back, tattoos spell his name.

His name is ATLAS.

Years ago, Atlas tried to destroy the LIBRARY OF DOOM.

The Librarian defeated him.

Then he was **buried** alive, deep
inside the earth.

He planned his escape for years.

Now, the giant is **free**.

He stares into the SKY.

He is searching for someone.

Atlas spies a tiny shape.

It is flying in the distance.

"YES!" says Atlas. "I knew he would come!"

The shape grows larger.

It **SWOOPS** above the waves.

It is the Librarian.

The Librarian hovers above the
WAVES. He points at the giant.

"You'll wish you never escaped
from your prison, Atlas!" he cries.

Atlas scowls. "You'll never
send me back!" he shouts.

The giant presses a finger against
one of his tattoos.

It is a letter. O.

The O flies off the giant's skin.

The O **SPINS**. It hums. It shoots through the sky.

It rushes toward the Librarian's head.

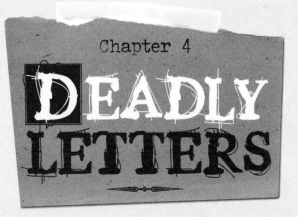

Chapter 4

DEADLY LETTERS

The Librarian snaps his fingers.

He **SPREADS** his hands apart.

The O starts to grow.

Soon, the Librarian can **pass** through it.

Then the letter turns into **SMOKE**.
It fades into the air.

"There's more where that came
from!" cries Atlas.

He presses another letter on his
arm. A giant X flies at the Librarian.

The X is a **MAGNET**. It pulls the Librarian onto its arms.

The Librarian cannot move.

The giant **jellyfish** glides toward the X. Long arms reach toward the Librarian.

"**One drop** of their poison, and you will be the Ex-Librarian," says Atlas.

The Librarian **CLOSES** his eyes. His glasses begin to shine.

Soon, his whole body **burns** brightly.

Flames burst from the Librarian.

The X **breaks**.

The jellyfish is blinded.

It flees to the bottom of the OCEAN.

The Librarian is free.

He **flies** toward Atlas.

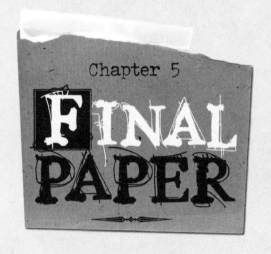

Chapter 5

FINAL PAPER

"Return these **BOOKS** to shore!" orders the Librarian.

"No. I don't care about them," says Atlas. "It is you I am after!"

A **LARGE** book floats beneath the Librarian.

Its covers slowly open.

The pages are wet.

The seawater has made them
SOGGY.

The Librarian cries out. He **falls**
from the air.

He lands on the wet pages of the
open book.

"I had many **YEARS** to think and plan," says Atlas.

"I learned everything I could about you and your Library. That's how I learned about your **WEAKNESS**."

"Wet paper," says the Librarian.

"You are **powerless** against it," says Atlas.

The Librarian sinks deeper. He is stuck in the slimy pages.

"Perhaps you need more C water," says Atlas.

He touches another tattoo.

The letter C leaps from his chest. It hangs above the Librarian's book.

The giant laughs. The C turns into water.

INKY rain spills onto the pages.

The Librarian cannot pull himself out of the black goo.

"Soon it will be all over," says the giant. "This is your last chapter. That book will be your <u>GRAVE</u>!"

The Librarian **SINKS** up to his chin.

WAVES splash onto the book.

The pages grow wetter and wetter.

Soon he will be **buried** in the paper.

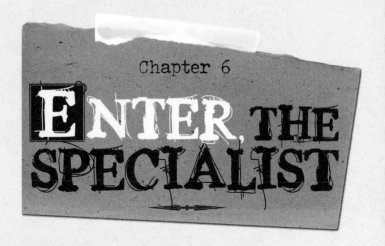

Chapter 6

Enter, the Specialist

Behind Atlas's head, another tiny shape flies in the distance.

The shape **GROWS** larger.

It **soars** above the waves.

The giant shouts, "How does it feel to be buried **ALIVE?**"

The Librarian's hand sticks out from the paper.

His **fingers** move weakly.

Suddenly, someone **swoops** down
and grabs the Librarian's hand.

He is pulled out of the book.

The Librarian looks **UP** at his
rescuer.

"The Specialist!" cries the Librarian.
"I thought you were just a **LEGEND**."

The Specialist smiles.

"Let's find out how **real** I am,"
she says.

"Specialist?" yells Atlas. "I will use your own **letter** against you!"

He touches a tattoo S on his arm.

The letter S grows into a **WHIP**.

The giant aims the whip at the woman. It wraps around her waist.

"Ah!" cries the Specialist.

She pulls the S whip off her waist.

Then she throws the letter back at the giant.

"Return to sender!" she says.

"NO!" screams Atlas.

The letter S wraps around Atlas's body.

Suddenly, he **SINKS** into the sea.

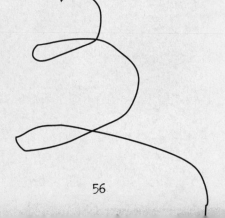

The Librarian turns to the
mysterious woman.

"So the legend of the Specialist is
true," says the Librarian.

The woman **NODS**.

"You protect the Books of Doom," she says. "I **PROTECT** the protector. You."

The Librarian looks around. He sees the floating books.

"I must return these books," he says.

"We'll need some help," says the Specialist.

She **CLAPS** her hands together.

The **SOUND** travels through the sea.

A herd of sea turtles paddles to the surface.

"Hardcovers," says the Specialist.

"They'll **FOLLOW** us."

The Librarian and the Specialist fly

to the Library.

Below them, the hardcovers — — — —

— —> **PUSH** the books back to shore.

AUTHOR

Michael Dahl is the author of more than 200 books for children and young adults. He has won the AEP Distinguished Achievement Award three times for his nonfiction. His Finnegan Zwake mystery series was shortlisted twice by the Anthony and Agatha awards. He has also written the Library of Doom series. He is a featured speaker at conferences around the country on graphic novels and high-interest books for boys.

ILLUSTRATOR

Bradford Kendall has enjoyed drawing for as long as he can remember. As a boy, he loved to read comic books and watch old monster movies. He graduated from Rhode Island School of Design with a BFA in Illustration. He has owned his own commercial art business since 1983, and lives in Providence, Rhode Island, with his wife, Leigh, and their two children Lily and Stephen. They also have a cat named Hansel and a dog named Gretel.

GLOSSARY

defeated (di-FEET-id)—beaten

destroy (di-STROI)—to ruin completely

gigantic (jye-GAN-tik)—huge or enormous

guard (GARD)—to protect from attack

hovers (HUHV-urz)—remains in one place in the air

legend (LEJ-uhnd)—a story handed down from earlier times

monstrous (MON-struhss)—horrible or scary

mysterious (miss-TEER-ee-uhss)—very hard to explain or understand

patrol (puh-TROHL)—to guard an area

pressure (PRESH-ur)—force produced by pressing on something

rescuer (RESS-kyoo-ur)—a person who saves another

terror (TER-ur)—very great fear

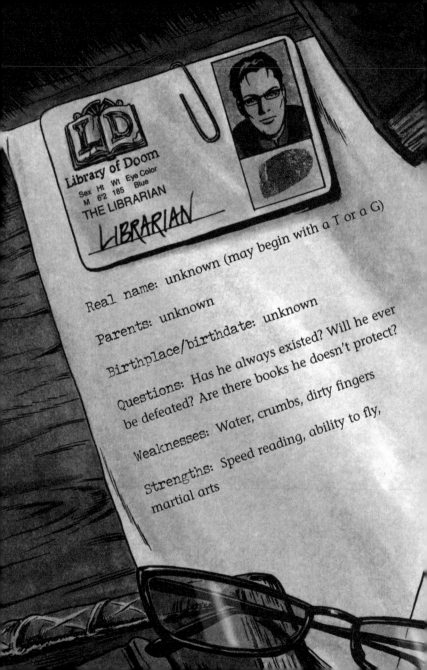

Library of Doom

Sex Ht Wt Eye Color
M 6'2 185 Blue

THE LIBRARIAN

LIBRARIAN

Real name: unknown (may begin with a T or a G)

Parents: unknown

Birthplace/birthdate: unknown

Questions: Has he always existed? Will he ever be defeated? Are there books he doesn't protect?

Weaknesses: Water, crumbs, dirty fingers

Strengths: Speed reading, ability to fly, martial arts

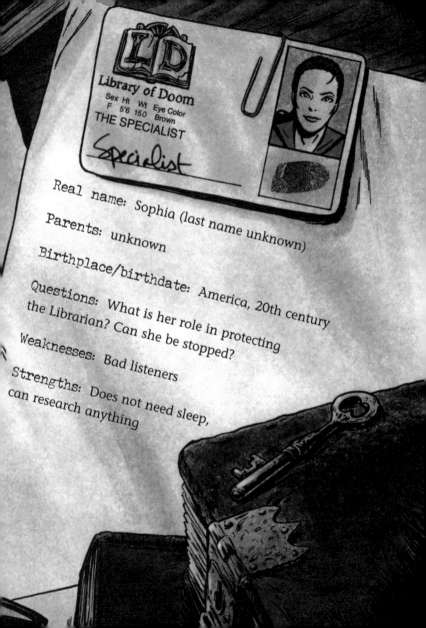

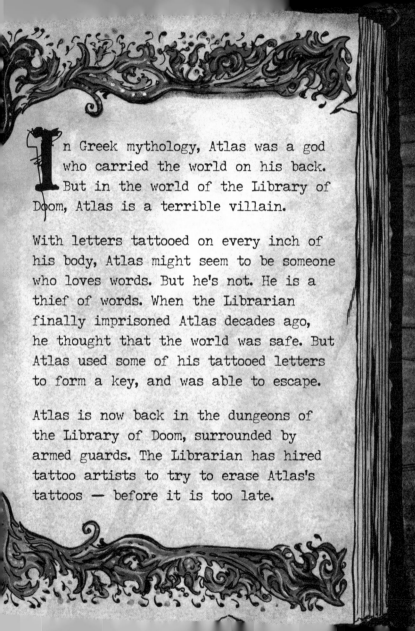

In Greek mythology, Atlas was a god who carried the world on his back. But in the world of the Library of Doom, Atlas is a terrible villain.

With letters tattooed on every inch of his body, Atlas might seem to be someone who loves words. But he's not. He is a thief of words. When the Librarian finally imprisoned Atlas decades ago, he thought that the world was safe. But Atlas used some of his tattooed letters to form a key, and was able to escape.

Atlas is now back in the dungeons of the Library of Doom, surrounded by armed guards. The Librarian has hired tattoo artists to try to erase Atlas's tattoos — before it is too late.

DISCUSSION QUESTIONS

1. Why did Atlas want to TRAP the Librarian?

2. What did you think about the title of this book? Does it match what you felt when you read the STORY?

3. Who is the Librarian? Who is the Specialist?

WRITING PROMPTS

1. Make a list of 5 letters that are **TATTOOED** on Atlas's body in this book. (Don't use letters that were mentioned in the story.) What does each tattoo do?

2. Part of the Library of Doom is underwater. What kinds of books do you think are stored there? What are they about? Make a list of titles of books that might be kept in the underwater part of the Library.

3. **CREATE** a cover for a book. It can be this book or another book you like, or a made-up book. Don't forget to write the information on the back, and include the author and illustrator names!